Po

I want to be the very best there ever was
To beat all the rest, yeah, that's my cause

Catch 'em, Catch 'em, Gotta catch 'em all

Pokémon I'll search across the land
Look far and wide
Release from my hand
The power that's inside

Catch 'em, Catch 'em, Gotta catch 'em all Pokémon!

Gotta catch 'em all, Gotta catch 'em all
Gotta catch 'em all, Gotta catch 'em all

At least one hundred and fifty or more to see
To be a Pokémon Master is my destiny

Catch 'em, Catch 'em, Gotta catch 'em all
Gotta catch 'em all, Pokémon! (repeat three times)

Can YOU Rap all 150?

Here's the rest of the Poké Rap.

Dratini, Growlithe, Mr. Mime, Cubone
Graveler, Voltorb, Gloom

Charmeleon, Wartortle
Mewtwo, Tentacruel, Aerodactyl
Omanyte, Slowpoke
Pidgeot, Arbok

That's all folks!

Words and Music by Tamara Loeffler and John Siegler
Copyright © 1999 Pikachu Music (BMI)
Worldwide rights for Pikachu Music administered by Cherry River Music Co. (BMI)
All Rights Reserved   Used by Permission

Collect them all!

Race to
Danger

©2017 The Pokémon Company International. ©1997-2017 Nintendo, Creatures, GAME FREAK, TV Tokyo, ShoPro, JR Kikaku. TM, ® Nintendo.

All rights reserved. Published by Scholastic Inc., *Publishers since 1920.* SCHOLASTIC and associated logos are trademarks and/or registered trademarks of Scholastic Inc.

The publisher does not have any control over and does not assume any responsibility for author or third-party websites or their content.

ISBN 978-1-338-17585-1

10 9 8 7 6 5 4 3 2 1   17 18 19 20 21

Printed in the U.S.A.   40
First printing 2017

Adapted by Tracey West

Scholastic Inc.

An Angry Challenge

"What's over that hill?" Ash Ketchum wondered.

Ash pushed back the red cap that he wore over his dark hair and squinted into the morning sun. He and his friends had been walking along a green, hilly path for hours. But now he could see bright bursts of color in the distance.

Brock shaded his eyes. "It looks like a bunch of hot air balloons," said the older boy. "Maybe it's some kind of festival."

"Cool!" said Misty. "Let's check it out."

Ash couldn't help smiling at his friends. Since his tenth birthday, Ash had been on a journey to catch and train Pokémon. Brock and Misty had been with him since the beginning.

Their journey took them all the way to the far-off Orange Islands. Brock had left them for a while to study Pokémon breeding with an expert named Professor Ivy. Ash and Misty decided to explore the Orange Islands on their own. They had some help from a Pokémon watcher named Tracey Sketchit.

Ash had many adventures on the Orange Islands. He saw strange new Pokémon. He captured a Lapras and a Snorlax. He even earned some new badges by battling Gym Leaders on the Orange Islands.

Now their Orange Islands adventures were over. Ash was sad to say good-bye to Tracey. But it was nice to be back with Brock again. It felt like old times. And Ash knew that Brock and Misty were usually up for anything.

"I'd love to see a balloon festival," Ash told them. "We need to take a break anyway."

"Pika!" agreed Ash's Pokémon, Pikachu. The small yellow Electric-type Pokémon had a tail shaped like a lightning bolt, pointy ears, and bright, red cheeks. Ash carried his other Pokémon in red-and-white Poké Balls.

But not Pikachu. It always walked alongside Ash.

Another that never traveled in a ball was Misty's Togepi. This tiny Pokémon hatched from an Egg, and still wore the eggshell around its little round body. Misty usually carried the baby Pokémon in her arms.

"These balloons are pretty amazing!" Ash said as they got closer.

Wicker baskets where passengers could ride were attached to the large balloons. Ropes attached to steel anchors in the ground kept the balloons from floating away. The balloons were lined up along a winding river.

Ash counted eight balloons. Each of them was

decorated with different colorful designs. A banner reading, Pokémon Balloon Race Today flew overhead.

The banner got Ash's attention. "Pokémon Balloon Race?" he wondered. "I've got to find out what this is about."

Spectators crowded the balloon field. Vendors selling souvenirs, food, and drinks were lined up on the north side.

Pikachu sniffed the air hungrily. Its stomach growled.

"*Pika?*" asked the Pokémon, pointing to a food stand.

"You're hungry now?" Ash asked. "Can't we look around a little first?"

Misty stepped up next to Ash. "I'm hungry, too," she said. "And so is Togepi. Why don't I take Pikachu and Togepi for a snack? We'll catch up with you in a few minutes."

"*Pikachu!*" Pikachu said happily.

"*Togi togi,*" gurgled the baby Pokémon.

"Good idea," Ash said. "Brock and I will take a closer look at some of the balloons. How about it,

Brock?"

Brock nodded. "Sounds good to me."

Misty took Pikachu's hand. Ash watched as they walked away and Misty's orange ponytail disappeared into the crowd.

"Which one do you want to check out first?" Ash asked Brock.

"How about that one?" Brock suggested. He pointed to a balloon decorated with an orange Pokémon that looked like a winged dragon. Ash recognized it: a Dragonite.

Standing next to the balloon was a girl about Brock's

age. She had long blond hair and wore a light-blue T-shirt and jeans.

Ash smiled. "I bet I can guess why you want to see that one," Ash teased his friend. Brock had a weakness for pretty girls.

Brock blushed. "Let's go," he said.

Ash and Brock approached the girl.

"Hi, I'm Ash," Ash introduced himself. "And this is my friend, Brock. Are you entering the race?"

Brock gave the girl his biggest smile. But the girl didn't smile back. In fact, she looked upset.

"I'm Windy," she said glumly. "I was in the race. But not anymore."

"What do you mean?" Ash asked. "What's wrong? Your balloon looks great."

Windy frowned. "It's not my balloon. It's my crew," she explained. "Each balloon needs at least two Trainers and two Pokémon to race. My brother Storm was going to ride with me. Last night, he was taking my Pokémon out for some exercise when they all fell into a pit in the field. They were all hurt, and now they're recovering in the Pokémon Center. I can't race without a crew."

Brock looked up at the balloon. "It's a shame. Your balloon is really nice."

"It's terrible," Windy said. "Now I won't get a chance to win Dratini."

Ash's eyes lit up. "Dratini? That Pokémon is really rare." Ash knew the small blue Dragon Pokémon was especially hard to find.

Ash took out Dexter, his Pokédex. The handheld computer had information about all kinds of Pokémon.

"Dratini, a Dragon Pokémon," Dexter said. "For years, people thought Dratini was just a myth. But a small colony was found living on the bottom of the ocean."

"That's Dratini, all right," Windy said. She sighed. "I've been searching for one ever since I got my Pokémon Trainer's license," she said. "This may be my only chance to ever train one. And now I've lost it."

"If it isn't Whiny Windy!"

Ash spun around at the sound of the loud voice. A teenage boy stood behind them with a mean look on his face. The boy had shiny black hair and wore a silver jumpsuit.

"Leave me alone, Jet," Windy said.

The boy sneered. "You were so sure you were going to win this race," Jet said. "And now you can't even get off the ground."

"I bet you're relieved," Windy shot back. "You know there's no way you could beat me."

Jet laughed. "Give me a break. You couldn't beat me if you were flying a rocket ship."

Ash didn't like this guy one bit.

"Hey, why don't you leave Windy alone?" Ash asked. He stepped up in front of the bully.

Jet glared at Ash. "Hey! Are you talking to me, pipsqueak?"

"That's right!" Ash said angrily. "And I'm no pipsqueak."

"We'll see about that," Jet said. He took a Poké Ball off his belt. "Let's settle this with a Pokémon battle!"

"You got it!" Ash replied. He was always ready for a Pokémon battle.

"How about one on one?" Jet asked.

Ash nodded.

Jet threw his Poké Ball in the air. "Fearow, go!" he yelled.

Who's Afraid of Fearow?

The Poké Ball burst open. White light flashed.

"Fearow!"

A Normal- and Flying-type Pokémon exploded from the ball, squawking and flapping its huge wings. The brown Pokémon had a long tan beak and savage-looking claws.

Ash knew that Fearow was hard to beat. It could fly in the air for a long time without having to rest.

But Ash was confident. He also knew that Fearow were weak against Electric-type Pokémon.

"Pikachu, I choose you!" Ash cried.

Ash waited for Pikachu's battle cry.

It didn't come.

"Uh, Ash," Brock reminded him, "Pikachu's with Misty, remember?"

Ash groaned. "I forgot." He had always counted on Pikachu when he went into battle. Ash had to change his strategy. What Pokémon could he use to beat Fearow?

"Bulbasaur, I choose you!" Ash cried, throwing a Poké Ball.

A Grass- and Poison-type Pokémon that looked like a dinosaur appeared. The blue-green Pokémon had a big plant bulb on its back. Ash had a lot of practice using Bulbasaur's attacks.

"Bulbsaur, use your Vine Whip!" Ash commanded.

"Bulba!" cried Bulbasaur. The tough little Pokémon opened up the plant bulb. Two long green vines shot out. They lashed at Fearow like two angry whips.

"Fearow, use your Agility!" Jet ordered his Pokémon.

Fearow swooped and dove in the air, dodging the vines with ease.

Ash knew he'd have to try harder.

"Bulbasaur, Razor Leaf!" Ash yelled.

A barrage of sharp green leaves flew out of Bulbasaur's plant bulb, headed right for Fearow.

Ash smiled confidently. The Razor Leaves always met their mark, and were always effective when they hit.

But Jet didn't look worried.

"Mirror Move, Fearow!" Jet called out.

Fearow flapped its wings and rose high above the attacking leaves. The leaves scattered harmlessly to the ground.

At the same time, Fearow flapped its wings some more. To Ash's amazement, sharp green leaves whipped up from the ground and headed right for Bulbasaur.

"Fearow is copying Bulbasaur's attack!" Brock warned.

Like Ash, Bulbasaur was too stunned to react quickly. The leaves smacked into Bulbasaur.

The Grass-type Pokémon was dazed, but not hurt.

But Fearow wasn't finished. It looked at Bulbasaur, a gleam in its eye. The Pokémon swooped down and picked up Bulbasaur in its sharp claws.

"No!" Ash cried.

Fearow flew up, up, up in the air.

Bulbasaur roared in protest, but Fearow didn't listen.

Ash didn't know what to do. Bulbasaur was helpless in Fearow's clutches.

"*Fearow!*" the Pokémon squawked, and then Ash swore he saw it smile.

Fearow released its grip on Bulbasaur in midair, sending the Pokémon hurtling down.

Crash! Bulbasaur slammed into the ground.

"Bulbasaur, are you all right?" Ash asked.

Bulbasaur groaned softly. It was okay, but in no shape to battle.

"Looks like I win!" Jet said smugly.

Ash sighed. "I guess so."

"And I'm going to win this balloon race, too!" Jet said. He looked at Windy. "Too bad your little friend can't help you."

Jet called Fearow back into its Poké Ball and walked off.

Misty walked up with Togepi and Pikachu. The two Pokémon were snacking on candy apples.

"Did I miss something?" Misty asked Ash. "It looked like there was a battle going on."

"There was, and I wish Pikachu had been here!" Ash said. "Why didn't you show up five minutes ago?"

"You could have beaten him without Pikachu," Brock said. "I've seen you beat guys like him before.

14

You should have called on Charizard."

Ash stomped his foot in the dirt. "Of course! Charizard is a Flying-type Pokémon, too. It would have been a better match," Ash said. "I don't know why I didn't think of it. I just got confused when I couldn't use Pikachu. And Jet was making me so angry."

Windy patted Ash's shoulder. "Don't worry about it, Ash. I have a hard time thinking clearly when Jet's around, too. He's good at psyching out opponents."

"I guess," Ash said. He introduced Misty to Windy and told Misty how Windy couldn't enter the race.

"It's too bad you won't have a chance to race Jet,"

Misty remarked. "I'd like to see somebody beat him."

"I would, too," Windy said. "But my brother was supposed to ride with me. So were my Vulpix and Butterfree. But they're all injured. I can't race without a crew."

"We could be your crew!" Brock said quickly. "You can borrow our Pokémon, too."

"Huh?" Ash said.

"Sure," Brock said, blushing. "I mean, if Windy wants us to."

Windy's eyes lit up. "Are you kidding? That would be great! Have you guys ever flown in a hot air balloon before?"

"Uh, no," Brock admitted. "But we're fast learners."

"That's good enough for me," Windy said. She turned to Ash and Misty. "Are you guys in?"

"Sure," Misty said. "It sounds like fun!"

"Count me in," Ash said. But to himself, he thought, *At least I'll have another chance to beat Jet.*

3

Ready, Set, Race!

"Great!" Windy said. "We'd better get ready."

Windy climbed into the basket.

"There are three major parts of a balloon," Windy explained. "The first part is this basket. That's where the passengers ride."

Next, Windy pointed to the balloon attached to the basket. "That part is called the envelope. When the air inside gets heated, it rises."

"How does it heat up?" Ash asked.

Windy patted a round platform in the center of the basket. "That's the third part," she explained. "Some balloonists use a burner fueled by propane. But in balloons like this one, a Fire-type Pokémon sits here and shoots flames up into the envelope, heating the air in there. Hot air makes the balloon rise."

"Okay, I get how the balloon goes up," Ash said. "But what makes it move forward?"

"Good question," Windy said. "I can't really steer the balloon. Wind moves it forward. But there are different layers of wind. So if I want to change direction or move faster, I can move up or down to find a layer of wind that will take me where I want to go."

Misty looked fascinated. "That's amazing! So how can we help?"

"Well, let's talk about Pokémon first," Windy said. "I used my Vulpix to heat up the balloon. Do any of you guys have a Fire-type Pokémon I could use?"

"You can use my Vulpix," Brock quickly offered. He opened up a Poké Ball, and a reddish Pokémon that looked like a fox popped out.

"Vulpix," squeaked the Pokémon in a high voice.

Windy examined the Vulpix. "This is a beautiful Pokémon," she said. "You've done a great job raising it."

"Thanks," Brock said, blushing again.

"My Vulpix was specially trained to fuel the balloon,"

Windy said. "Do you think yours is up to the challenge?"

Brock nodded. "You can count on it."

"Great!" Windy said. "I have to replace my Butterfree, too. I need a Pokémon that can fly ahead and test the air currents for me."

Ash threw a Poké Ball in the air. A Normal- and Flying-type Pokémon with brown-and-white feathers appeared in a burst of light.

"How about my Pidgeot?" Ash asked.

"Perfect!" said Windy.

Ash smiled, happy that Pidgeot was on his team. Not long ago, Pidgeot had left him to help some other

Flying-type Pokémon that needed it. Pidgeot rejoined Ash when he returned from the Orange Islands, and he was glad to have it back.

"What about us?" Brock asked. "Can we ride with you, too?"

"Misty and Ash can ride with me," Windy said. She turned to them. "You can help me direct the Pokémon, and you'll be here to back me up in case anything happens."

"Pika?" Pikachu asked.

Windy laughed. "You too, Pikachu."

"What about me?" Brock asked eagerly.

Windy fished into her pocket and pulled out a set of

car keys. She tossed them to Brock.

"See that van over there?" she asked, tossing her head.

Brock nodded.

"I need you to be my chase crew," she said. "Follow our route on the ground. When it's time to land, make sure the landing site is clear. Think you can handle that?"

"Sure," Brock said, but Ash knew he was disappointed not to ride in the balloon with them.

Brock brightened a little, though, when Windy explained that he'd be in constant contact with them thanks to a radio in the van.

"We can do this," Ash said. "I can't wait for this race to start!"

At Ash's words, a voice blared over a microphone.

Ash looked. A woman in a blue suit stood on top of a platform.

"All contestants for the balloon race please enter your balloons," the woman said. "Starting time is five minutes."

Ash, Windy, Togepi, and Pikachu took their places inside the basket.

"Welcome to the Pokémon Balloon Race," said the announcer. "Each of our balloon teams are made up of Trainers and their Pokémon. Let's meet the teams!"

Ash snapped to attention. He was curious to see what kinds of Pokémon the teams were using. "First, we have Team Jet," said the announcer. Ash looked at Jet's balloon. It had pictures of three winged Pokémon on it: a Venomoth, a Fearow, and a Scyther. Two boys in leather jackets shared the basket with Jet. A Charmeleon fueled the balloon. Jet's Fearow sat on the balloon basket, ready for action.

"Next is Team Poké Ball!"

Their balloon was designed to look like a giant Poké Ball. The team's Fire-type Pokémon was a Charmander, and its Flying-type Pokémon was a Pidgey.

"In spot number three, we have Team Farfetch'd!"

This balloon was painted with a Farfetch'd, a Flying-type Pokémon. A real Farfetch'd was on the crew, along with a Vulpix.

"Vulpix are popular with many hot air balloonists," Windy explained.

"Next, Team Midnight!"

This team's balloon looked like a night sky, with a moon and stars. Instead of a Fire-type Pokémon, the balloon was powered by a propane burner. Clefairy, a friendly pink Pokémon with pointy ears, worked the burner. A Zubat waited in the Flying-type Pokémon position.

"Team number five is Team Jigglypuff!"

This balloon was bright pink, and was painted to look like a Jigglypuff. A real Jigglypuff worked the propane burner. A Spearow circled the balloon, waiting for the race to start.

"Team Golbat is number six!"

A large painting of a Golbat, a Flying-type Pokémon that looked like a fierce blue-and-purple bat, decorated the sixth balloon. A real Golbat hung upside down from the bottom of the balloon. And Growlithe fueled the balloon envelope.

"In the number-seven spot, Team Meowth!"

This team's balloon had the face of a Meowth, a Scratch Cat Pokémon, on it. Inside the balloon basket were two people wearing goggles, caps, and scarves around their necks. A Meowth in goggles worked the propane burner. Weezing, a Poison-type Pokémon that looked like a cloud, floated alongside them.

Misty nudged Ash. "Doesn't Team Rocket travel in a Meowth balloon?" she asked.

"Yeah," Ash replied. A trio of Pokémon thieves known as Team Rocket was always chasing them and trying to snatch Ash's Pikachu. "But their balloon blew away the time they chased us over that snowy mountain, remember? And besides, that doesn't look like Team Rocket. The announcer said they were called Team Meowth."

Misty shrugged. "I guess you're right. But it seems kind of suspicious to me."

The emcee pointed to Windy's balloon. "Finally, we have Team Dragonite!"

Ash waved to the crowd as they cheered and clapped. He smiled and turned to Windy. She looked happy and confident.

The emcee continued. "The test balloon we sent out earlier landed at the foot of Ariel Mountain," she said. "The captain of the first balloon to reach the landing spot there will win the grand prize."

The woman motioned to the river.

"Dratini!" she called out.

The river water began to ripple. A blue-gray head shyly emerged from the water.

The Pokémon slowly rose up and began to swim on the surface of the water. It had a smooth body with a long tail and large ears. Dratini did a happy flip in the water as the crowd cheered.

"Wow!" Ash said.

"It's beautiful," said Misty.

"And it's going to be mine," Windy said. "Thanks to you guys."

The woman on the platform held a starter pistol in the air.

"Ready, everyone," she said. "On your mark, get set, go!"

4

An Angry Challenge

Brock untied the anchor ropes.

"Now, Vulpix!" Windy commanded.

Vulpix shot a stream of fire up into the balloon. The envelope began to swell with hot air.

Ash looked anxiously at the other balloons. Some of them were filling up faster than Windy's. Jet's balloon was even starting to lift off the ground.

"Can't we do this any faster?" Ash asked Windy.

"Don't worry, Ash," Windy said. "Vulpix is just warming up. But I know it's going to do a great job."

Jet's balloon started to soar away.

"So long, losers!" Jet called to them.

"We're right behind you!" Ash yelled. "Just you – whoaaaa!"

The balloon lurched and began to rise into the air. Misty held Togepi tightly.

Brock ran to the van and started the engine.

"See you at the finish line, Brock!" Ash called out. Misty and Togepi waved to Brock.

One by one, the other balloons lifted off. A light wind kicked up, and they all glided across the field.

Ash looked down. The people in the crowd looked smaller and smaller.

"This is awesome!" Ash exclaimed, as the cold wind stung his cheeks. "We're gonna win this race. I know it!"

Ash wasn't the only one feeling confident.

Across the field, the crew of Team Meowth cheered and clapped.

There was a teenage girl whose long red hair was tucked into her flight cap.

There was a teenage boy whose green eyes peered out from behind his goggles.

And there was Meowth, a white Pokémon dressed like a pilot.

It was Team Rocket, of course! This trio of Pokémon thieves was always up to no good.

Today was no different.

Jessie, the girl, waved at the crowd below.

"These disguises are genius," she said.

"No one would guess that we're really the cleverest Pokémon thieves around," added James, the boy.

"*Meowth!* You can say that again," said Meowth, the Pokémon.

Jessie took out a pair of binoculars and eyed the Dratini. "I can't wait until we win that Dratini," she said greedily. "The Boss will be so pleased when we bring it to him."

"It will make up for the utter humiliation we suffered the last time we brought him a Dratini," James said.

"Yeah," added Meowth. "It turned out to be a double-crossing Ditto instead."

"It would be so nice to have a real Dratini," James said with longing.

Jessie grinned. "We'll get it, thanks to my plan. Digging that pit outside Windy's campsite was a brilliant idea. Windy was the favorite to win the race. Without her crew, she can't race, and we'll win for sure!"

Meowth nudged Jessie. "Uh, isn't that Windy over there?" The Pokémon pointed to the balloon with the Dragonite painted on it.

Jessie scowled. "How is she flying without her Pokémon?"

James focused the binoculars on the balloon. "Oh, no!" he cried. "I don't believe it!"

Jessie grabbed the binoculars. "Give me those!" she snapped. She looked at the balloon. Then she gasped.

"It's that troublemaking twerp, Ash, and his high-flying friends!" she cried. "They're going to ruin everything."

"Drat!" James said. "I thought we were going to sail off into the sunset. But now we'll just be blasting off again!"

"You sound like a *balloon-atic*!" Meowth said. "This is just what we need."

Jessie's eyes lit up. "You mean . . ."

Meowth nodded. "That's right. If we make sure Windy's balloon goes down, down, down, we can escape up, up, and away with Pikachu!"

"And then we'll be poised to win the Dratini!" James added.

"What are we waiting for?" Jessie asked. She took out a Poké Ball.

Windy's balloon was starting to fly past Team Rocket's balloon.

"Just a little closer," Jessie said.

"Here, balloon," coaxed Meowth. "Nice balloon."

As if obeying their command, Windy's balloon floated closer to them.

"Arbok, go!" Jessie yelled. She hurled a Poké Ball through the air.

A huge Pokémon that looked like a hooded purple cobra appeared in a blaze of light. Arbok had sharp

fangs and a dangerous poison sting.

"Arbok, take down that balloon!" Jessie said.

Arbok whizzed across the sky. It opened its mouth and bared its long fangs.

Suddenly, a gust of wind sprang up.

Windy's balloon surged forward.

Team Jigglypuff's balloon floated in front of Arbok.

Arbok couldn't control its flight path. It collided with the Jigglypuff balloon.

"Jiggly! Jiggly!" The Jigglypuff inside the balloon pointed and cried out in alarm.

Arbok's fangs ripped into the nylon envelope, tearing open a jagged hole in the top of the balloon.

"Arbok, return!" Jessie cried.

"Fangs a lot, Arbok!" Meowth said.

The Pokémon disappeared back into its Poké Ball.

But the crew of the Jigglypuff balloon wasn't so lucky. The balloon slowly sank to the ground as the air leaked out of the hole.

"No fair!" James said. "That should have been Windy's balloon."

But Jessie smiled an evil smile. "It doesn't matter," Jessie said. "We've just eliminated part of the competition. One down, six more to go!"

5

Beedrill Attacks

"What's happening behind us?" Misty asked.

Ash spun around. Team Jigglypuff's balloon was slowly sinking to the ground.

"They're falling!" Ash cried. He turned to Windy. "Can we help them?"

Windy shook her head. "I'm not sure what went wrong," she said. "But these things happen all the time. It's part of the sport. It looks like they've got it under control, though. They'll land safely."

Windy picked up the radio receiver.

"What happened to the Jigglypuff crew, Brock?" she asked.

"They're okay," Brock replied. "Looks like a safe landing."

"Great," Windy said. "Over."

"Over," returned Brock.

"That's good," Ash said, but for the first time, he felt a little nervous. From a distance, balloon racing looked like fun. Now that he was in the thick of it, he realized how dangerous it could be.

Windy saw his worried look. She smiled. "Relax, Ash," she said. "We're going to be fine. I've been flying these things since I was a little girl."

"Really?" Misty asked. "How did that happen?"

"I grew up on Ariel Mountain," Windy said. She pointed ahead. Ash could just see the mountain's tall peak behind cotton-candy clouds.

Windy continued. "I lived up there with my parents. They were balloonists, and loved to be close to the sky," Windy said. Then her voice trailed off. "But it was lonely sometimes."

"Didn't you have any friends?" Misty asked.

Windy shook her head. "Not really. I used to sit outside and stare at the clouds," she said. "I learned a lot about Flying-type Pokémon that way. And then one

day I saw the most beautiful Flying-type Pokémon of all." She looked up at her balloon.

"You mean a Dragonite?" Ash asked.

Windy nodded. "It flew past the clouds one day. I had to rub my eyes. I thought I was dreaming."

"So that's why you want to win the Dratini," Misty realized.

"Yes," Windy said. "I'll devote my life to raising that Dratini. If I'm lucky, it might evolve into Dragonair. And then, finally, Dragonite."

"That would be awesome," Ash said. He remembered when his Caterpie evolved into Metapod, and then finally a beautiful Butterfree. It was an amazing experience.

Windy smiled. "I'll take such good care of that Dratini," she said. Then she looked out at Jet's balloon. Her face clouded. "I can't say the same about Jet. He's pretty tough on his Pokémon. That's another reason why I want to win this race."

Ash saw that Jet was still ahead of them. "Is there anything we can do to catch up?"

Windy motioned to Pidgeot. "Can you send out Pidgeot? Maybe there's a faster current we can try."

"Sure," Ash said. He told Pidgeot what to do.

"Pidgeot!" The Flying-type Pokémon flew off the balloon, soaring high into the sky. Then it circled back and swooped down, below the balloon. Finally it landed back in the basket.

"Pidgeot, Pidgeot," squawked the Pokémon.

"Pidgeot says there's a fast current about ten feet below us," Ash told Windy.

"Excellent!" Windy said. "Vulpix, lower your flame a little."

The Fire-type Pokémon obeyed. Slowly, the balloon started to drop.

"This is a nice current," Windy said. "If we're lucky, we can ride it all the way to Ariel Mountain."

Ash relaxed a little. Windy sounded confident. The sun was shining. And below, Ash saw that they were flying over a field of colorful flowers. Wild Butterfree twirled and dipped in the sky below them.

Ash took a deep breath of the cool air. He checked out the other racers. Now Windy's balloon had a slight lead over the rest, although Jet's balloon was close behind. The other balloons were keeping up, too.

Then Ash felt something pulling on his leg. Pikachu

was trying to get his attention. The Pokémon's pointy ears were twitching.

"*Pikachu! Pika pika!*' Pikachu said worriedly.

Ash looked around. Everything seemed normal.

"Pikachu, what is it?" Ash asked.

Then he heard it. A low buzzing sound. The dense hum was growing louder and louder.

"Do you hear that?" Ash asked his friends.

Windy leaned over the balloon basket.

"Could be trouble," she said calmly.

Ash followed her gaze. It looked like some kind of blanket was rising above the flower field. A buzzing, humming blanket.

The blanket rose higher and higher into the sky. Now Ash could make out shapes. Black-and-yellow shapes with red eyes, gray wings, and sharp stingers.

"It's a swarm of Beedrill!" Ash yelled, shocked. There were hundreds of them.

"They must be attracted to the bright colors of the balloons," Misty said.

Now the swarm started to fly sharply into the sky. In perfect formation, the Beedrill headed for the balloon shaped like a Poké Ball.

Ash watched in horror as the Beedrill covered the top of the balloon. The red-and-white balloon was now black and yellow.

A loud hissing sound filled the air.

"The Beedrill have punctured the other team's balloon!" Misty cried.

As the balloon deflated, it slowly sank down to the field of flowers.

The Beedrill rose up from the damaged balloon. Now they took aim at Team Golbat's balloon.

The crew screamed and tried to frighten the Beedrill away.

It didn't work. Once again, the Beedrill covered the top of the balloon.

Hisssssssss! The balloon started sinking to the ground.

The Beedrill flew off the Golbat balloon in perfect formation. They took aim once again. But who would be their next victim?

Ash tensed as hundreds of red beady eyes focused on the Dragonite balloon.

"Windy!" Ash cried. "They're coming right for us!"

6

Watch Out for Weezing

"Those Beedrill are angry now," Windy said. "I don't think they're happy about the balloons popping on them."

The angry buzzing was growing closer and closer.

"Can we fly away from them?" Misty asked Windy.

Windy shook her head. "The current we're riding isn't fast enough for that," she said. "I don't think there's time for me to find something faster. But maybe we can rise above them. Vulpix, turn up the heat!"

Vulpix shot a higher, brighter stream of flame from its mouth.

It was too late. The swarm of Beedrill passed Jet's brown-and-green balloon. They turned their sharp tails toward Windy's bright orange balloon.

"I can't get out of the way!" Windy cried.

An idea flashed into Ash's mind. He quickly grabbed a Poké Ball from his belt and threw it in the air.

"Squirtle!" Ash yelled. "I choose you!"

A Pokémon burst out of the ball. Squirtle, a Water-type Pokémon that looked like a cute turtle, was ready for action.

"Blast those Beedrill!" Ash commanded.

Squirtle hopped up on the edge of the balloon basket. It faced the attacking Beedrill and shot a forceful stream of water from its mouth.

Misty threw a Poké Ball, too.

"Starmie, help Squirtle!" she cried.

A starfish-shaped Pokémon appeared. Starmie shot a water blast out of one of its pointy arms.

The two blasts of water knocked the Beedrill backward. They struggled to stay in flight.

"Finish it, Pidgeot!" Ash yelled. "Use Gust!"

The Flying-type Pokémon flew up to the swarm and furiously flapped its wings. A strong gust of wind swirled in the air.

The wind gust picked up the swarm of Beedrill. In a flash, they went flying across the sky, far away from the field.

"Good job!" Ash hugged his Pokémon.

Windy, Misty, Pikachu, and Togepi all joined in a cheer.

The radio crackled. "Are you guys all right?" Brock said. "It's hard to tell what's going on up there."

Windy quickly told Brock how they got rid of the Beedrill.

"Great job, guys!" Brock said. "Over and out."

"Big deal!" Jet called over from his balloon. "So you swatted a few bugs! Anyone could do that!"

"Oh, yeah?" Ash yelled back. "I didn't see you doing anything."

Misty put a hand on Ash's shoulder. "Don't waste your energy on him," Misty said. "You did great and you know it."

"Yeah," Windy said. "You kept us in the race. Jet's only mad because we're still in the lead."

"I guess," Ash muttered. But deep down he was fuming.

Now he wanted to beat Jet worse than ever!

Over in the Meowth balloon, Team Rocket watched Beedrill's assault with glee.

"Beedrill usually drive me buggy," Meowth said.

"But they just did us a big favor."

"Too bad that annoying little twerp Ash didn't get stung, too," Jessie said.

"We'll take care of Ash," James said. "Pikachu is as good as ours!"

"Don't be an airhead," Meowth snapped. "We're stuck in last place!"

Jessie scowled. But Meowth was right. There were still four balloons ahead of them: Team Midnight was closest. Then came Team Farfetch'd, Team Jet, and Windy's balloon, Team Dragonite.

James turned to the Poison-type Pokémon at his side. Made of toxic gas, Weezing had two heads, both with sick expressions on their faces.

"I can fix that," he said. "Go, Weezing!"

48

"Weezing," groaned the Pokémon.

"Weezing, Smog that balloon!" James pointed to Team Midnight's balloon.

Weezing flew over to the balloon. Three teenage girls made up the crew. A Clefairy worked the burner.

Weezing blew a puff of poison gas into Clefairy's face.

"Clef clef clefairy!" coughed the gentle Pokémon. It toppled off the burner.

"What's going on?" the girls yelled. "Zubat, Wing attack!"

The crew's Zubat flew down from its perch. The blue-and-purple Pokémon circled Weezing. Then it slapped the Poison-type Pokémon with its powerful wings.

The attack had little effect on Weezing.

"Weezing, Weezing," the Pokémon belched. Thick clouds of smelly black smog poured from its body.

Zubat fainted from the poison, falling on top of Clefairy. The girls coughed and choked as they struggled to get to the burner.

But the poison smog rose up and filled up the inside of the balloon, pushing out the hot air. Without the hot air to inflate it, the balloon started to collapse.

The girls fell to the floor of the balloon basket, still coughing from the putrid smog.

Team Rocket watched as the balloon sank to the ground.

"Weezing, return!" James called.

Weezing flew back to the balloon basket. Jessie, James, and Meowth looked at one another and grinned.

"All this success is wonderful!" James said. "I feel like I'm floating on air!'

Jessie smacked him on the head. "You are floating on air, dimwit!"

"But soon we'll have our feet on the ground," Meowth said. "We're getting closer to the finish line."

"And closer to catching Pikachu!" said Jessie.

7

A Sudden Storm

"Look over there!" Misty cried. "I think Team Midnight's balloon is going down!"

Ash leaned over the basket. The withered balloon spiraled slowly to the ground.

Ash wasn't sure, but he thought he saw trails of black smog following it.

He grabbed the radio receiver. "Hey, Brock," he said. "Did you see what happened to that balloon?"

"I didn't see the whole thing," Brock replied over the radio. "But that smog looks a little suspicious to me. Over."

"That's just what I was thinking," Ash said. "It looks

like a Poison-type Pokémon was behind this somehow. Over."

"I'll see what I can find out down here," Brock said. "Over and out."

Windy listened to their conversation. She frowned. "I can't believe somebody would resort to using their Pokémon against the other racers," she said.

"Why not?" Ash asked. "Somebody sabotaged your crew, didn't they?"

Windy didn't reply at first. Then she took a deep breath. "We can't worry about that now," she said. "We've got to focus on the race. Ash, Misty, what does it look like out there?"

Ash turned around. "Jet's balloon is closing in on us," he reported. "It looks like he's taking his balloon a little higher."

"He must be trying a different current," she said. "Keep an eye on him for me."

"Right!" Ash replied.

"Team Farfetch'd is about one hundred yards behind Jet. Its balloon is riding in a lower air current," Misty added.

Windy nodded. "Okay."

"And then there's just one balloon left," Ash said. "Team Meowth. They're riding at about the same level we are."

"They could still be a threat," Windy said. "But right now I'm most worried about Jet."

Ash looked at Jet's balloon. It was about thirty feet above them now. And it looked like it was gaining speed.

Windy still seemed confident, though. She stared at Ariel Mountain, which looked a lot closer than it did when they had started.

If Windy can be confident, so can I, Ash decided.

A strong gust of wind kicked up behind them.

The balloon lurched forward. Ash had to grab onto the side of the basket. Pikachu clutched his pant leg. Misty clutched Togepi and sat down on the floor.

Ash held onto his cap with his other hand to keep it from blowing off.

"Hey, this is great!" Ash yelled over the roar of the wind. "This wind will get us there fast!"

Windy shook her head. "This can only mean one thing," she said. She looked up at the sky.

Ash followed her gaze. Thick gray storm clouds were

racing across the once-blue sky. A low rumbling sound filled the air.

"We're in for a storm," Windy said. "It'll be fast, but furious!"

The wind kicked up even more. The balloon rocked back and forth in the sky.

Lightning flashed in the distance, followed by a loud crack of thunder.

"What do we do?" Ash called out.

"Hold on tight, and hope that it's over soon!" Windy yelled back.

Ash huddled next to Pikachu and Misty on the floor of the basket. One by one, cold raindrops hit his cheeks.

Then something hard and sharp hit his leg.

"Ouch!" Ash cried. He reached down and picked up an icy piece of hail.

"It's hailing!" Ash yelled over the roaring wind. "Can the balloon take it?"

"The balloon is made of nylon," Windy said. "It's pretty strong. But I'll see if I can get us out of the storm's path."

Windy stood up. "Vulpix, can you try a hotter flame?"

"*Vulpix,*" replied the Pokémon bravely, but Ash saw

that it was having trouble keeping its balance.

Ash took out a Poké Ball.

"Bulbasaur, hold on tight to Vulpix!" he said, when the combination Grass- and Poison-type Pokémon appeared.

Bulbasaur moved quickly. It sent two vines out of its plant bulb. They wrapped around Vulpix, holding it steady.

The other balloons were getting blown around as badly as theirs. Hail slammed against the tops of the balloons.

Suddenly the crew of Team Farfetch'd began to shout. Ash saw that the hailstones had ripped a hole in

the very top of the balloon.

Windy noticed it, too. "They must be racing in an older balloon," she said. "But these hailstones are pretty big. They could damage just about anything."

"Even this balloon?" Ash asked.

Rat-a-tat-tat! Hailstones smacked into their balloon, as if answering his question.

Behind them, the Farfetch'd balloon started to sink to the ground.

Rat-a-tat-tat! More hailstones assaulted Windy's balloon.

"It's much too dangerous up here," Windy said. "We're going to have to land!"

Prepare for Trouble

Ash sprang into action.

"Just keep steering us out of the storm," Ash told Windy. "I'll take care of the hail."

"I trust you, Ash!" Windy replied.

Ash held up a Poké Ball.

"Charizard, I choose you!" Ash cried.

A large Pokémon exploded from the Poke Ball. Charizard looked like a huge lizard with wings and a flaming tail. The combination Fire- and Flying-type Pokémon flapped its wings in the air just outside the balloon basket.

"*Char!*" roared Charizard.

"Charizard, melt that hail!" Ash commanded. "Save the balloon!"

For a second, Charizard hesitated. Ash froze. Would his Pokémon obey him?

Then stinging hailstones slammed into Charizard. The Pokémon roared angrily as it flew up above the balloon. It opened up its mouth and shot a huge blast of fire up into the sky.

The hailstones melted before they hit the balloon, turning into harmless raindrops just in time.

"Keep it up, Charizard!" Ash yelled.

While Charizard worked above the balloon, Windy worked with Vulpix and Pidgeot to steer the balloon into a lower, faster current. Vulpix struggled to keep a bright flame going. It was getting harder and harder for the little Pokémon to keep up. But it did. In seconds, the storm was behind them.

"We did it!" Ash yelled triumphantly. "Charizard, return!"

A light flashed, and Charizard disappeared back into its Poké Ball.

"Good thinking, Ash," Misty said as she stood up. "It's lucky that Charizard finally learned to obey you."

"It didn't take that long," Ash said, frowning. Actually, it hadn't been easy getting Charizard to listen to him. He made a lot of mistakes along the way. But now that he and the Pokémon understood each other, they made a great team — most of the time.

"That was great, Ash," Windy said. She picked up the radio. "Brock, can you give me a report? Over."

Brock's voice crackled over the radio receiver.

"There are only two teams left besides you," he said. "Team Meowth and Team Jet. Jet has a slight lead. Over."

Windy gazed out at the sky.

"He's going strong," she remarked. "But this race isn't over yet."

"One more thing," Brock said. "I talked to the crew of Team Midnight. Ash was right about that smog. They say a Weezing attacked their balloon. Over and out."

"A Weezing attack?" Misty said. "That sounds like Team Rocket to me."

"I don't know," Ash said. "Team Rocket isn't smart enough to sabotage a whole balloon race."

"Don't be so sure of that!" a voice cried.

Ash spun around. Team Meowth's balloon was right behind them. The voice belonged to a girl in an aviator's outfit – goggles, a cap, and a scarf. A teenage boy and a Pokémon dressed like aviators stood next to her.

Suddenly, the girl took off her cap to reveal long red hair.

"Prepare for trouble!" she said.

The boy and girl took off their outfits to reveal white uniforms underneath. Each uniform was emblazoned with a red letter R.

"Make it double!" said the boy.

"Team Rocket!" Ash cried.

The Pokémon thieves laughed. Jessie and James launched into the Team Rocket chant:

"To protect the world from devastation,
To unite all peoples within our nation.
To denounce the evils of truth and love,
To extend our reach to the stars above.
Jessie!
James!
Team Rocket – blast off at the speed of light.
Surrender now or prepare to fight."

"*Meowth!* That's right!" finished the Scratch Cat Pokémon, taking off its goggles and scarf.

Misty groaned. "I'm so sick of that chant," she said.

"And I'm so sick of you!" Ash told Team Rocket. "What are you up to now?"

Jessie smiled an evil smile. "We're about to make sure you don't win this race."

Windy glared at Team Rocket. "Why don't you play by the rules, like the rest of us?" she asked. "I've trained hard to get into this race."

"Stop complaining," James said. "If you had stayed on the ground like you were supposed to, we wouldn't be threatening you now."

Windy's face clouded with fury. "You mean you're the ones who dug that pit and injured my crew?"

Meowth chuckled. "They fall for it every time!"

Windy approached Pidgeot. "I'm going to get us away from these clowns before I do something I regret," she told Ash and Misty. "Pidgeot, find us a way out of here!"

"Not so fast!" Jessie said. She threw a Poké Ball. "Arbok! Go!"

James threw a Poké Ball, too. "Weezing! Go!" he cried.

Arbok and Weezing burst out of the Poké Balls. They paused in midair, waiting for orders.

"Those dimwitted dreamers think they can win this race," Jessie said. "Arbok, it's time to burst their bubble!"

"Weezing! Use Smoke Screen so we can get Pikachu!" James ordered.

Arbok and Weezing flew over to the balloon. Arbok sank its fangs into the side of the envelope.

"Oh, no!" Ash yelled.

"It's all right, Ash," Windy called to him. "We can still fly with a hole in the side of the balloon. Only a hole in the top of the balloon can ground us."

Jessie heard her. "Higher, Arbok!" she commanded her Pokémon.

Arbok flew to the top of the balloon.

At the same time, Weezing flew into the basket. Puffs of smoke started to pour from its body.

Hisssss! Arbok was puncturing a small hole in the top of the balloon.

"We've got to stop them!" Windy yelled.

Blast Off, Bad Guys!

Ash looked up at Arbok, then down at Weezing. Who should they stop first?

Then Ash knew what to do.

"Bulbasaur! Squirtle! I choose you!" Ash cried, throwing two Poké Balls at once.

The Pokémon appeared in the balloon basket.

"Bulbasaur! Vine Whip!" Ash yelled.

Two vines lashed out of Bulbasaur's back. One shot up outside of the balloon, encircling Arbok. The other reached up and grabbed Weezing.

Ash knew he had no time to lose. The Pokémon wouldn't be held back by the vines for much longer –

especially not Weezing, who was hard to hold onto in the first place.

"Squirtle! Bubble Beam!" Ash shouted.

Bulbasaur held Arbok and Weezing outside the balloon. Squirtle opened its mouth and aimed big, strong water bubbles at the two Pokémon.

One bubble encased Arbok. Weezing got trapped in another.

"Let go, Bulbasaur!" Ash cried.

Bulbasaur released its grip. Then it reached its vines up to the two holes in the balloon, plugging them with leaves.

At the same time, Arbok and Weezing floated in the air.

Ash knew that the wind would send them right back to Windy's balloon. He had to blow them away. But how?

Just then, Pidgeot flew back to the balloon, ready to report to Windy.

"Pidgeot! Gust!" Ash told the Flying-type Pokémon.

Pidgeot flapped its wings, sending a strong blast of air at Arbok and Weezing.

The gust sent Arbok and Weezing floating back to Team Rocket's balloon.

Arbok's bubble popped right on top of the balloon. Arbok crashed into the balloon, ripping a huge hole with its sharp fangs.

Weezing's bubble popped inside the basket. Startled, the Pokémon released a huge cloud of thick black smoke.

Team Rocket's balloon began to deflate.

"I've got a sinking feeling we're about to blast off," James moaned.

"*Meowth!* This balloon race is a bust," Meowth added.

Ash turned to Pikachu. "Let's give them a shocking send-off!"

"*Pika pika!*"

Pikachu concentrated all its energy into a big electric charge.

"Pikachuuuuuuuuuuuuu!" Pikachu cried, aiming the sizzling blast at Team Rocket.

Jessie, James, Meowth, Arbok, and Weezing screamed in surprise as the electricity coursed through the balloon.

"So long, losers!" Ash called out.

The deflated balloon spiraled wildly across the sky.

"Looks like Team Rocket's blasting off again!" the Pokémon thieves cried.

Ash turned to Misty and Windy. "We did it!" he cried.

But the two girls looked worried.

"We haven't won this race yet," Windy said. "Bulbasaur can't keep those holes covered much longer." she said.

Bulbasaur was determined to keep its vines up in the air, but Ash could see that Windy was right. The Pokémon was weak from the effort.

"Not only that," Misty said, pointing. "But thanks to Team Rocket, Jet now has a big lead!"

Ash looked. Jet's balloon soared about fifty feet in front of them.

"That Dratini is as good as mine!" Jet shouted back at them.

10

Charizard Heats Things Up

"We've got to repair that leak!" Ash told Windy. "We can't lose this race!"

Windy forced a smile. "Looks like you want to beat Jet almost as much as I do," she said. "But I don't know what to do. I'm out of ideas."

Misty opened up her backpack. She took out a pack of chewing gum and tossed it to Ash.

"Maybe this will help," she said.

Ash caught the gum, puzzled.

"This is no time for snacks, Misty," Ash said. "We've got a real problem."

But Windy brightened. "Great idea, Misty," she said.

"Ash, get Bulbasaur to shoot out some Razor Leaves."

Ash hesitated. Then he realized what the girls were thinking.

"Right!" Ash said. "Bulbasaur, how about a few leaves?"

"Bulba!" said the Pokémon. Some wide green leaves gently floated out of Bulbasaur's plant bulb.

Ash put several sticks of gum in his mouth and began to chew. When the gum was nice and sticky, he took it out and attached it to the leaves.

"Pidgeot! Fly up there and fix that leak!" Ash told the Normal- and Flying-type Pokémon.

Pidgeot squawked. It picked up the leaves in its beak. Then it flew to the top of the balloon and dropped the sticky leaves on top of the puncture Arbok had made.

"All right!" Ash cheered. Bulbasaur dropped its vines, relieved.

"That takes care of our first problem," Misty said. "Now we just have to catch up to Jet."

Ash looked up. Jet's balloon was traveling on a swift current, high above them.

"If we can get up there, we might catch up to them," Ash said.

"No problem," Windy said. She turned to Vulpix.

The small Pokémon was trying its best to produce flames, but it looked weak and tired.

"Oh, no," Windy said, stroking the Pokémon's fur. "Vulpix has been working too hard to keep this balloon afloat. I don't think it's got much more to give us."

Windy sadly stared at the mountain. "I guess Jet's going to win this race after all."

But Ash wasn't ready to give up.

"This isn't over yet!" Ash said. He threw a Poké Ball outside the balloon. "Charizard, I choose you!"

The big Fire- and Flying-type Pokémon appeared alongside the balloon.

"Charizard, we need some fire power to get this balloon going," Ash said.

"Char?" Charizard didn't seem happy to be given such an ordinary job.

"Please, Charizard," Windy pleaded. "Vulpix has done its best. But we need a powerful Pokémon to finish the job. We can't win this race without you!"

Charizard's face softened. It gently picked up Vulpix in its mouth and deposited it in Windy's arms. Then it hopped up onto the platform.

Charizard roared loudly, then shot a stream of flame up inside the balloon.

Whoosh! The hot air quickly filled the balloon. The balloon started to rise higher and higher.

"Keep it coming, Charizard!" Windy called to the Pokémon. She was smiling broadly now.

The balloon rose up and up. Suddenly, Ash felt a strong current push them forward.

"We found the current!" Windy said. "Tell Charizard to keep it steady. We don't want to go any higher."

"Char!" The Pokémon heard Windy and lowered its flame a little bit.

Now they were right behind Jet's balloon.

"Hey, Jet!" Ash called out. "Maybe you won't get that Dratini after all!"

Jet spun around. A look of anger and shock clouded his face at the sight of Windy's balloon.

"I thought you were out of the race!" he yelled.

"Not by a long shot!" Ash yelled back.

Jet waved his arm, and his Fearow flew to his side. Then he yanked two Poké Balls off his belt. He threw them in the air.

"Scyther! Venomoth! Fly!" Jet cried.

The balls exploded in a blaze of light, and when the light faded, two Pokémon flew in the sky alongside Fearow.

Scyther was a combination Bug- and Flying-type Pokémon with razor-edged wings that looked like sharp swords.

Venomoth, a combination Bug- and Poison-type Pokémon, had purple wings and big, blue eyes.

"Scyther, Venomoth, Fearow!" Jet screamed. "Tear that balloon to bits!"

Flight to the Finish

"That's cheating!" Windy yelled angrily.

"Too bad!" Jet said. "We're too far up for the ground crew to see us. It'll be your word against mine. As far as I know, some wild Pokémon attacked your balloon."

The Scyther flapped its wings and flew toward Windy's balloon. Ash had seen Scyther in action before. His friend Tracey had one. Ash knew how fierce they could be.

Fearow swooped down from the sky. Ash had already lost to it once. Could he beat it this time?

The Venomoth flew right behind it. This Pokémon worried Ash, too. He knew its potent poison attacks could paralyze everyone on the balloon. Ash quickly reviewed his Pokémon. He had to think of a battle plan fast.

"Bulbasaur, take Fearow. You can do it this time," Ash said.

"Bulba!" Bulbasaur said with determination in its voice.

"Squirtle, wash away any poison Venomoth tries to use," Ash told the Water-type Pokémon.

"Squirtle!"

"Starmie!" Misty called. "Help Squirtle!"

Ash turned to Pikachu. "Pikachu, stop that Scyther!"

"Pikachu!" Pikachu nodded confidently. It hopped up on the edge of the basket.

Ash's Pokémon sprang into action.

Bulbasaur lashed at Fearow with its Vine Whips, giving the Flying-type Pokémon no time to launch a counter-attack.

Squirtle soaked Venomoth with a steady stream of water.

Scyther let the other Pokémon battle. It flew to the top of the balloon, ready to slice the envelope wide open.

"Piiiiikaaaaaaaaaaaa!" Pikachu concentrated all of its energy into a forceful electric attack. Lightning bolts sprung from its red cheeks. They sliced through the air and sent an electric charge through Scyther's body.

"Scyyyyy!" Jet's Scyther somersaulted through the air. Then it steadied itself. It looked at Pikachu angrily.

"Scy! Scy!" Scyther forgot about the balloon. It flew up to Pikachu, slicing the air with its razor-sharp wings.

"Pikachu, watch out!" Ash cried.

Pikachu hopped back into the basket, narrowly avoiding Scyther's attack.

"Good job, Pikachu!" Ash said. His heart beat wildly. His Pokémon were doing great!

Suddenly, the balloon dipped in the air.

"What's happening?" Ash cried.

"It's Charizard," Windy said, pointing. "Look!"

Charizard flew off the plattorm. It roared angrily at Scyther.

Ash gasped. Charizard had never liked Tracey's Scyther. The Fire- and Flying-type Pokémon was probably eager to battle this one.

"Charizard, no!" Ash yelled. "We need you to fuel the balloon."

Charizard ignored Ash. It aimed a red-hot flame at Scyther.

The Bug-type Pokémon ducked the blaze.

"Don't worry about those Pokémon!" Jet told Scyther. "Take down the balloon, and you'll take them all down!"

Scyther flew away from the balloon, then looped around to build up momentum. It flew toward the top of the balloon with super speed.

Charizard started to take off after it.

But before it could, a soft cry came from the platform.

It was Vulpix. The Pokémon weakly struggled to shoot another flame into the balloon.

Ash could see Charizard was torn. It knew Vulpix wasn't strong enough to keep the balloon in the air. But it didn't want to give up its battle with Scyther, either.

"Charizard, keeping the balloon in the air is the most important thing you can do right now," Ash said.

Charizard didn't make a move.

"Pika pika chu! Pika chu!" Pikachu told Charizard. It moved its arms excitedly.

"What did Pikachu say?" Windy asked.

"Pikachu told Charizard that it would beat Scyther," Ash said. "Pikachu will defend the honor of all the Pokémon in the balloon. But they'll all lose unless Charizard fuels the balloon."

Charizard nodded to Pikachu. Then it stepped back up on the platform.

"All right!" Ash said. "Pikachu, you'll need help.

Pidgeot, you know what to do."

Without hesitation, Pidgeot flew next to Pikachu and lowered its back. Pikachu hopped on, and Pidgeot flew out of the basket and up to the top of the balloon.

Scyther hovered above the envelope, poised to strike.

"Pikaaaaaaa!" Pikachu let loose with a powerful Thunder Wave. A huge burst of electricity illuminated the sky.

The charge passed through Scyther's body. Fearow and Venomoth were caught in the blast, too.

Scyther toppled off the balloon, weakened. Fearow and Venomoth couldn't flap their wings. Quickly, Bulbasaur used its Vine Whip to catch the Pokémon. Then it threw them back into Jet's balloon.

Scyther wasn't the only one affected by the Thunder Wave.

Pikachu and Pidgeot were thrown back by the blast. Ash reached out over the basket.

"Gotcha!" he cried, catching the Pokémon in his arms.

The force of the Thunder Wave also pushed the balloon ahead, like an airplane using its engines to thrust forward. In one fast blur, Ash saw them zoom past Jet's balloon.

Finally, Windy's balloon slowed down. Ash looked behind him.

Jet's balloon was a speck in the distance.

"Ariel Mountain!" Windy cried.

Ash turned around. The tall mountain peak towered in the sky just ahead of them.

The radio crackled. Then Ash and the others heard Brock's voice.

"I almost lost you guys," Brock said. "What happened up there?"

"It's a long story," Windy replied. "We're about ready to land. How does it look down there? Over."

"The test balloon landed in a field behind a red farmhouse," Brock said. "Can you see it? Over."

Ash looked over the basket. The bright red farm-house was easy to spot in the green field.

"We've got it," Windy said. "We'll see you soon, Brock! Over and out."

"Over and out," Brock said.

Windy turned to Ash. "Charizard can take it easy now," Windy said. "We're coming in for a landing."

Compared to the hectic race, Ash thought landing was a piece of cake. Windy and Charizard worked together to carefully control the amount of hot air in the envelope. The orange balloon slowly and gracefully sank down onto the grassy field.

A crowd of people cheered as the balloon hit the dirt. Brock ran up to them. In the excitement, Ash and Misty started to talk at the same time, telling him what he had missed on the ground.

The contest announcer walked up to Windy.

"Congratulations!" she said, handing Windy a Poké Ball. "You'll need this for your new Dratini."

Windy stared at the Poké Ball as if she didn't believe it was real. Then she climbed out of the basket.

Dratini was swimming in the river right next to the landing site. Windy walked up to the riverbank.

The Dratini shyly looked at Windy. Windy smiled and waved.

"I'll take good care of you, Dratini," Windy said. "I promise."

Dratini smiled and jumped out of the water, happily splashing its tail.

Windy turned back to Ash and his friends.

"I couldn't have done this without you," she said. "Thank you so much! I'll never forget you."

Windy hugged them all. Brock blushed bright red.

"I'm glad you won Dratini. It seems to really like you already," Ash told Windy. "And I'm really glad we beat Jet!"

"Ash, you won a lot more than a race," Brock said.

"What do you mean?" Ash asked.

"When you lost that battle to Jet, your confidence was shaken," Brock reminded him. "Jet rattled you. But in that race, you made some great decisions. You used your Pokémon in creative ways. I'd say you won your confidence back."

Ash beamed. "I guess you're right!" Ash said. "You know, I never really lost my confidence. I've always known I have what it takes to be a Pokémon Master."

Misty groaned. "Thanks, Brock. That's just what Ash needs — more confidence."

Ash ignored her. He picked up Pikachu.

"Pikachu knows what I'm talking about," Ash said. "Together, we'll take on any challenge that comes our way. Right, Pikachu?"

"Pikachu!"

About the Author

Tracy West has been writing books for more than twenty years. She enjoys reading comic books, watching cartoons, and taking long walks in the woods (looking for wild Pokémon). She lives in a small town in New York with her family and pets.

Next in this series:

Talent Showdown

The stage is set for an explosive Pokémon Talent Showdown! There's a juggling Exeggutor, a singing Charmander – even a dancing Farfetch'd. Ash wants to beat Gary but he doesn't have an act. And that's not all he has to worry about. Team Rocket's grand finale has the audience glued to their seats and all the Pokémon under their spell! It's curtains for the Pokémon – unless Ash can steal the show.